Prologue

*Unki

The wind whipped viciously, dragging my heavy wings as I flew over the sea.

Of course, we won't remember this tomorrow, the sweet time we spend soaring higher than the clouds and dipping our toes in the sea. That is something that never transpires. I will continue to protect us, to hide us and to contain the boundaries of our magic. But, what if it's not enough? What if I go too far and I can't come back from the edge? It's not always enough just to know who you are, having others around who truly see you is an experience I dream about every day. I always see them out there in the village, I watch how they interact, love, fight and play. Unfortunately, I have never and will never know what that is like.

But at least I'm not completely alone. Not really.

Elle

I'm always picked last, overlooked.

But somehow, when I beat them all to the ground, they are convinced that I cheated. I will never be good enough in their eyes, maybe in anyone's eyes. Even the people I trust, they don't seem to stand up for me, not when it matters anyways. Just once, I really wish I could come first, be seen as the strong person that I truly am and be able to finally show them – show myself. I want to know what else is out there, what is beyond the vast sea. Are we alone, trapped on this little island, that we call home?

Unknown

She almost caught me today, every fibre of my being tells me to just go to her, tell her who I am. What we are to each other. But I can not put her through this, such an unfortunate fate. I will watch her, protect her from a distance. Maybe, just one day I won't have to feel so alone.

Chapter 1

They call me Ghost.

My pale complexion and odd demeanour have only led to the rest of the village mocking me. But if that group near the shoreline does not scram, I will be giving them a mouthful. That would be sure to hurt their ego's, they would never recover if me, the tiny little pale girl beat them up and sent them home crying to their warrior fathers. Well, I'm a warrior too. They would probably lie though, just tell people that Fester did it. He often gets the credit for the solving of my misfortune, but at least I still get some hits in. My reputation within this village is clearly not reputable, but at least I have Fester, my best friend. Right now, I just need to swim in the sea with him, to relax.

As soon as Fester looks at the others, they all run away, except for the gaggle of girls who hang around ogling him. Why wouldn't they? He looks like a Greek god. Damn son of a warrior! Fester Terra Goldhelm, if he wasn't my best friend, I would think him a pompous idiot.

"Any sign of that dragon last night?" he asked in that silky voice of his.

Shaking my head, I tread the water waiting for him to join me. Heat from the morning sun kissed my chilly skin, small bumps raced up the length of my arms, the water rippling around me.

"Hey 'Ter Bear, do you think I'm odd?" Losing himself within the water, he splashed me gently. A few droplets touched my cheek, sliding smoothly down my skin.

"Of course I do, Elle. Still, is there anyone that I need to beat up for you?" he chuckled, but there lingered a serious edge.

Floating on his back, he listened as I told my tale of woe. A story I had told numerous times before, ever since I was small. He always tried to help fight my battles for me, but still stood surprised when I took control of the situation myself every time. "You know I can handle myself in a fight... no matter what those losers believe."

"The village Elders still won't allow you to become a recognised warrior, I assume?" questioned Fester. We had floated out to the deeper water whilst we spoke, shaking my head to his question, he opened his arms to me with a look of pity upon his face. I debated smacking that look straight off his handsome, chiselled face. But instead, I accepted his offer and hid my small body within his arms. Taking my fingers, I traced one of the many scars on his arms – the marks of a true warrior. I had never been granted permission to fight against the Dark One, my father had believed in me, so why won't they?

He easily held me, treading the water as his bright green eyes scanned the sea. His looks were damn supernatural compared to me. My weird silver eyes and hair were no comparison when it came to his bright green eyes and brown hair. His muscles… Every girl in our village openly admires him, whereas every guy in our village openly ignores me.

"They say because I haven't faced the dragon on my watch – and because I am a girl – I cannot have the title. Yet, half the men, even those a rank lower than me, have received it. They did nothing to gain it, I don't see them protecting the entire village at night whilst everyone else sleeps!" I sighed, my head falling against his shoulder. He ran his hand through his hair, slicking it back. I felt every movement of his powerful muscles, that's something I've not managed to figure out yet, no amount of training or stuffing food in my mouth has granted me use of my muscles. Am I a little bit faster? Sure.

"They don't see your strength yet, Elle, but they will. Besides, we've never had an attack at night; it's just a precaution." He added. But I know exactly what he isn't saying.

Mumbling under my breath, I pushed away from him and engaged him in his competitive side. It wasn't like us to sit around and talk about our feelings, we are warriors, that's just not something we do.

Drying off in the morning sun, I feel my eyes starting to flutter closed. "Not here you don't," he whispered, his words floating into my mind, as I drifted away. The dream or rather, the nightmare began like the rest, blood splattered across the walls and Fester stood over me, his arms reaching desperately. But his face, something on his face made me cower away. I would never leave him behind, there is nothing he could do or say that would make me betray him. Still, this girl in the dream who pretends to be me – she is terrified of him. Subconsciously, scared that the blood on his hands could be her own.

"Elle!" Mum's frightened voice broke the seal behind my eyes. "I'm ok," I croaked, accepting her soft fingers as she pulled me up. "Do you think the nightmares will ever stop?" she asked, the sheets pulled tight beneath me as she sat down. Shrugging I leant against her warm shoulder. It's been a year, and still, this is the most communication I can ever pull from her. Dad's death broke her completely; this is something I don't think she will ever truly heal from. None of us will. The other women in the village had formed a group, they like to sit together making and mending clothes, talking about the harvest. I forced her to join, watching her slowly come back to life, just enough. At least, now she has some company, other than me.

She hated that I decided to follow in my father's footsteps, and I often found her asleep in the chair, waiting for me to return home in the morning.

She doesn't seem to worry when I am with Fester, which just gives Fester and I an excuse to spend more time together. Even if the dreams that currently plagued me were full of lies, using his face to scare me. What a scam, my 'Ter bear would never hurt me. The only thing he does want to hurt is that dragon.

We all have our own personal vendettas against it. Our warriors grow stronger each day and our hunting team is getting closer to the answers that we need. Well, that's what the village Elders say, anyways. I'm not sure I trust a single word that comes out of their wrinkly old mouths. I've had twenty-five years of practice in this village; no one and nothing is ever as it seems. The village Elders make up the oldest heads of all the families – the original settlers on this land.

Only the Elders know our true histories, and they hold the records of it. Still, we blindly follow them. Every sunset I sit and eat dinner with mum, thinking about dad and questioning our very existence. All whilst the thirst for revenge boils in my blood and keeps me awake at night. Even though the encounter would be horrible, a part of me hopes the stupid dragon appears whilst everyone else is asleep. That way when I am the one to kill it, no one can say any different, I can revel in their shock. Not to mention I can finally put an end to that monster's reign. For almost my entire life, that creature has disrupted our peace, scared our livestock and stolen our lives. I'm ready for all of that to end.

Chapter 2

Slowly, I collected my things and said goodbye to my mother. To dear old Rose, it was the small things, like the goodbyes that meant more to her now than ever before. Every single one is a reminder of who we have lost and how quickly life can change.

"Hey Fester, have you started your watch already?" I asked, perching on the rocks beside him.

"Keiran had to head home early. Why did you miss me?" He teased, then took a small package out of his pocket and offered it to me. Popping the sweet candy in my mouth, the sweetness sliding along my tongue as I said,

"I need to hunt down some more charcoal, I've run out. Can't sketch without it!"

He sighed, clearly not onboard with me going alone. Probably annoyed that I hadn't made the trip with him this morning, as I should have.

The vast forest separated the village from the mountains, the known home to the dragon – even though we had no idea where the actual nest lay. It seems every time that our warriors tracked down some clues as to where it may be hiding, they somehow lose it again. Either they are just very stupid, or this dragon is much smarter than we planned for. Many attacks ago, I suggested that a group follow the damn thing home, but apparently that is too dangerous. Wouldn't it be more dangerous to not act now, instead allow it to keep killing us? To keep taking our food. Not that the village Elders ever suffer.

"Fine. If you insist on going out there, at least strap your sword on properly," he said.

Fester's voice cut through my deep thoughts, with a roll of my eyes, I turned and backed in between his thighs. His strong and gentle hands reached around me as I passed over the sheaths and straps.

Fester began by wrapping the bottom strap around my waist, the metal buckle scraping as he threads the pin through the hole and tightens the leather. It rested comfortably as his hands slid expertly up my sides, grabbing the middle strap. The leather now pulled tight under my breasts, the metal cool through my shirt as his skilled fingers worked the straps. Gentle arms reached around, hugging me from behind as Fester wrapped the last strap around the top of my chest.

My breath hitched as calloused fingers brushed the nape of my neck. "You look good in leather," he whispered, reaching for the sword in my hands.

Slowly he stepped back and I felt the heavy blade slide in between my shoulder blades. "Thank you," I finally breathed.

His smug face finally came into view, I really would love to smack that smile right off his face. Fester ran his hand through his hair, looking me up and down, and sighed, "Ok, be careful and stick to the trail."

I rolled my eyes, my fingers resting against the side of his face, "don't worry 'Ter bear, I'll be fine, I will be on my best behaviour and look out for any danger that may come my way."

Giving him a quick kiss on the nose, I laughed as he swatted me away. Sliding my hand from under his chin, I picked up my sketchbook and sauntered away into the gloomy forest.

If I don't pass the dead trees and I stick to the ruins of the old village, then I should be safe. But we can never predict when the Dark One will strike, his presence thankfully keeps away other strange creatures – that we know of.

The leaves crunched underneath my shoes, the damp earth spilling in through my worn soles. The ice-cold wind kissed the nape of my neck, I watched as the sky grew darker with every passing minute. I should hurry, my shift was due to start soon, whilst the rest of the village danced by the firelight and kissed their children goodnight. My nightly ritual of sketching under the moonlight was a relaxing and peaceful moment to myself that I thoroughly enjoyed. Sometimes, Fester would join me, keeping me company silently, whilst the night air whistled past us, and the stars created an atmosphere like no other.

Kneeling I brushed my long fingers through the long grass – searching, I had to pretend I was looking for something in case I was caught in the act.

The village within the forest, or the remaining ruins of the village, was the place I went for my charcoal at first, but it has been a hot minute since there was any left here. I hated to use it, but I needed it. Thankfully, ashes from a warm fire worked just as good, so I had back up options if I couldn't find any.

The final ray of sunshine sank below the horizon, this was my sign that if I didn't move soon, then Fester would be coming to find me. Sighing deeply, I turned around and started heading out of the forest, a sharp crack to the left of me had my head whipping round, I peered through the trees trying to see what it could've been. I knew it would not be Fester, he would not come that way, but I could not see anything or anyone else.

This village was our history, a history we did not remember, we had no idea what happened here or what happened to the people that once lived here. Why would they abandon it?

Our little seaside village was all that was left of the settlements on this island, we were a simple community with a one-track mind. Right now, it was to stay alive. The dragon threatens our already limited numbers every single day. I turned away again, walking back to the place I had left Fester.

As I stepped out from under the trees, I saw Fester standing there with the firelight dancing in his eyes, lost in his thoughts as he sharpened his sword. The warmth from the fire spread through my body, sliding up my arms and tingling down my spine. I could already envision the drawing I would be committing myself to tonight. He had the heart of a warrior, but his mind was that of an explorer, always looking for an adventure.

The sea in the background called to him and the fire created pictures of love and wonder.

When he keeps me company his patience rarely ever lasts the whole night, most likely we will get to hour three and then he will start begging me for attention. He is a child at heart. But I love him; he is my family. Our friendship confuses everyone else, but to us we make sense. That's what matters the most.

"Any luck?" he asked, hand running through his hair as he made room for me on the log he was currently sitting on. The bark creaked and shifted underneath my weight, coming to rest comfortably between my legs. Facing him, I shook my head and pulled out what little I had left, it would be enough till morning when the ashes from the fire would finish the remainder of the sketch.

"Were you alone in the forest?"

"It was as quiet as can be," I lied.

Muttering under my breath about the damp grass, I stuck out my hand and adjusted his chin, positioning him perfectly for my sketch. The firelight glinted in the emerald of his eyes. "Better?" he smirked, and my heartbeat quickened.

That's when we heard the dragons cry.

Chapter 3

This was strange, the dragon never struck at night, it was unheard of. The luminescent moon had reached its highest peak in the night sky, I could hear the flap of the beast's huge wings coming towards our peaceful village. The warriors piled into the centre of the village, their weapons ready and all our resources were being protected. I sighed, there goes my peaceful night, after this attack we would be rebuilding all night that's for sure.

This is finally my chance to show everyone what I am capable of, I would not be forced to stay away from this battle. They had no excuse as to why I should not be able to defend my home and people.

As I dragged the blade from its holster upon my spine, the light from the moon bounced off the blade's edge, illuminating Fester's back who stood in front of me. The wind rolled off the dragon's back as it emerged from behind the safety of the trees, "We will not lose each other tonight." This was the mantra we stuck behind any time an attack happened, and we would continue to do so until this monster was defeated.

The archers lifted their bows towards the sky whilst the swordsmen readied themselves on the ground. Fester and I joined them, sweat sliding across the back of my neck, my nerves were shot. Fester ran his hand through his hair, brushing it out of his eyes, I still didn't understand why he didn't just chop it all off.

My long braid tucked nicely into the straps of my sheath, providing me with full visibility, my eyes were so used to darkness after so many night shifts. I had the better advantage compared to the others, I could finally prove myself not only to my peers but also the Elders, as they cowered in their homes watching through the slit of their door. Calling them the village Elders was laughable, the youngest one was only thirty.

"Get ready! It's coming around. Archers on my mark!" Our leader gave the commands, shouting as the wind picked up again. Shadows danced across the low-lying clouds, the air filled with smoke as the Dark One released his flame and gave away his position. Our leader signalled and the archers fired instantly.

Fester suddenly grabbed me, whilst pushing a few of the others out of the way, as we all ducked for cover behind our stone defences. We made it in the nick of time as the Dark One roared out, all the pain and anger heard in its deep roar unleashed as his flame burned the grass where we once stood. The ground cracked under the pressure. Looking through the smoke, black scales came into view, the ground shuddered beneath us as four huge feet suddenly slammed into the ground.

My eyes caught one of the dragon's own eyes; it was large and unyielding. I froze in my step, my whole body felt paralysed. Waves upon waves of emotions struck me, thankfully Fester didn't even notice, he raced forward with the others to attack the dragon. I was lost in my subconscious, by the time I regained the ability to move the battle was over with, the dragon was wounded in the fight, rising into the air it changed direction and disappeared into the night sky.

There were no tragedies tonight, the village barely shook by the attack, this didn't seem right to me. It just left us with more unanswered questions. Everyone remained on high alert, expecting it to come back any minute, but somehow, I just knew that it wouldn't. Fester remained near my side; he was always so protective of me. My peaceful night was already ruined by the dragon's appearance, so now I would stay up sharpening my sword and practising my swing ready for the next opportunity.

"Don't you think we should go out there? Follow it home and attack whilst it is unprepared, not to mention, wounded." I demanded, my rage barely under control as the men laughed at my expense. "Look," Fester said, pulling me into his chest, "I know this must be difficult for you, but this is how it works. We follow orders – not make them up, okay?" I nodded even as my brain came up with a plan. If they are not going to be smart or brave enough to do this, then I will. Or at least stupid enough that is. Sometimes I don't understand Fester, he can do anything but instead follows like a sheep. I thought he would want to eliminate this huge threat that took so many of our families' lives away.

Why did the dragon just come here? Why did it not fully attack anyone and why are there no buildings on fire? It was all confusing, not to mention my own reaction to the dragon was the biggest mystery. I turned and walked away from the other warriors, peering into the forest. Just on the other side of these tree's is the green lake and beyond that are the mountains. If I went towards the mountains, it wouldn't take me too long to hopefully find the dragon's nest. I could easily go alone...

Hands suddenly grasped my shoulders, tightening around me. "I know that look, the tension in your shoulders. Don't even think about it Elle." His voice had dropped low, warning me to stay away from this.

He pulled me in for a cuddle, attempting to soothe me but all it did was show me the challenge ahead. The challenge against him, the warriors and the village Elders. They would see the saviour that I am, if I came back with the dragon's head in tow. "But 'Ter bear…" I whined, appealing to his playful side.

Spinning myself in his arms, I held his eyes whilst I wrapped my arms around his neck. He huffed and rolled his eyes, one hand brushing away that glorious fringe of his. "My little Ghost…" He sighed, pressing his soft lips to my forehead and hugging me around my hips. My senses consumed him as our bodies pressed so tightly together. "What will it take to make you stay?" he asked, "can I convince you?" I giggled at his efforts of persuasion. "That stuff might work on your other conquests, Fester, but you know it doesn't work on me, but nice try."

Chapter 4

Fester turned and walked away from me, reporting to our leader, whilst I stood around waiting for my replacement for the day. It had taken him three hours of holding me in place to convince him that I wasn't going to do something completely stupid. All the while, in my head I was planning to do exactly that.

My eyes quickly zoned into the distance as long legs came into view, along with a snarky look on her face. Arabella, not someone remotely important but someone who hates my guts because of my relationship with Fester. No one understands that we are just best friends, and nothing more will ever come of that, that was a mutual agreement.

Walking back home, the mud cracked under the pressure of my feet. Mum was expecting me home, and Fester expected me to stay there till evening until our swimming date. This means I had all day to track the Dark One, by sneaking away. "Something on your mind dear?" Mum asks, noting my ulterior motive the second I walked through the door.

"Just tired Mum, I think I will take most of the day to rest. It was a big night."

"Of course, honey, I won't disturb you. Just let me know if you need anything," she replied. Worry was wrinkled across her forehead. I know she had been watching, she always did, staying up most nights in her chair, anxious that I wouldn't come home, just like my dad. With a kiss to her cheek, I retreated into my room and set the plan into motion.

Covering my pillows with sheets and planting my spare shoes in front of the bed, I hopped straight out of the window. In the low morning sun, the grass crunched beneath my feet. Thank God! That I am so vigilant as it allowed me to take in my surroundings easily, not to mention most people were still asleep so this was the perfect time to sneak out. I flew straight into the forest, taking quick cover behind the trees.

If I was caught by the ruins, I would have an explanation, that I was exploring. But anything past that, I'd not have much luck coming up with a reasonable excuse, and it's not like my feminine wiles would get me anywhere as I simply did not have any.

The smell of the fresh moss and pine gradually started to fade, this was my first sign that I was entering forbidden territory.

The Dead Forest, so named by the lack of life in anything around us. The trees laid broken, there was no wildlife, or even footprints around. The earth was so hard, it didn't even register my existence as I skulked my way through. Suddenly pain shot through my calf, a sign I had twisted my ankle, after I almost tripped over a large rock half buried under the stiff clay.

"Idiot…" I muttered to myself, turning my leg this way and that as I began to put pressure on it. Hissing, I hobbled over to the closest tree, the bark stabbing me in the shoulder. The cold wind drifted past me, allowing goosebumps to erupt up both of my arms, a couple more steps ahead and my ears perked up. I could hear water rushing.

There were stories once upon a time that the water near our village had healing properties, perhaps it could help me now. Or at least provide me a safe resting place.

The breeze guided me towards the lurid lake, with each step I took, the pain in my foot increased, my vision blurring. I probably should've headed home but instead I kept on with my adventure. I slipped my foot out of my shoe exposing it to the mid-morning air, the coolness of the wind making my foot throb.

Hopping the rest of the way from soft soil to the sandy edge of the water side. I was mesmerised, the water had an almost soothing feel to it like it was inviting me in, promising comfort within its presence. The water was not blue, instead lime green, it must've been from the limestone and wildlife nearby. I dipped my toe in, checking the temperature before fully submerging both feet. The thick cool liquid bubbled and erupted in a kaleidoscope of colour as my skin went deeper and deeper.

I looked towards the mountains, not far from where I stood, thinking to myself how close I could be to the dragon right now. It could be hiding behind, above or even below but if I don't find it today, I will come back every day until I do find it – "What the hell?"

Panic flooded through me, the tide had suddenly turned, instead of relief from the water it was replaced with searing pain. The water seemed to be suckling on to every piece of skin it could touch, and no amount of shaking seemed to discourage it. My feet continued to sink; the suffocating aqua taking control of my body.

Over the gurgling of the water, I could hear voices whispering. The lake was speaking to me, trying to entice me to stay and swim. It seemed to have a paralysing effect on my body, as I could no longer fight my way out of the water. I felt my body being dragged under, spinning into a whirlpool closer to the centre. The numbness did not just affect my body but also my mind, I suddenly felt relaxed, I could stay in this water forever. Watch the clouds float by and listen to the wind as it whistles through the cracks in the great stone mountains. Maybe the dragon would join us, the water could subdue the flame that pains him. I think he would like that. It's been quite some time since Emmet had graced these waters with his presence.

I groaned, the liquid filling my ears as my head slowly started going under. "Emmet…" A voice whispered in my mind.

Who is Emmet? My conscience had awoken itself; I was finally able to move and speak. "Help! Somebody please, help me. Help!" I yelled, until the searing liquid trickled down my throat. I choked on the water, trying my best to call out, to make any discernible sound in hopes someone nearby would come to my rescue, but it was to no avail.

My head jerked under, my eyes closing as the last bit of my oxygen was sucked from my lungs. This was it. I always thought I would die at the paws of the dragon, or even one of its kin after I brought it down. Instead, I'm to be defeated by water.

All I can think about is Fester, he's going to be angry that I left and even more angry when he realises, I'm never going to return. He will try to find me; he won't be able to though. I once imagined a life with him, we could've been happy together.

My love for him goes deeper than the sea we share, further than death can carry me away and yet, a small part of me that still clings to hope, is relieved that I won't have to face that day when it finally comes.

Chapter 5

I heard the crackling fire first.

The dark embers flickering behind my sensitive eyelids as I finally came to. Something was telling me not to open my eyes. I was slowly trying to piece together what happened, my memory failing me. The only thing I did know was that whoever saved me, it was not Fester, from the lack of angry arms around me. So... somehow a stranger managed to pull me from that death trap lake. How... I don't know. I must proceed with caution.

"Or you could just open your eyes and say thank you." The gruff voice startled me, I inhaled sharply choking as smoke filled my lungs.

Moonlight greeted me as my eyes fluttered open, my vision hazy and my mind still dizzy.

A male form slowly came into view, starting from the floor I raised my eyes, limb by limb his figure came into focus. Reaching his eyes, I sucked in a breath, he had the most beautiful blood red eyes. It wasn't uncommon for people to have alarming eye colours, but I had never met anyone with red eyes before.

"Well now you have. Here… this water is safe to drink," he said, muttering as the glorious male specimen slid a wooden cup my way.

My whole body screamed in pain as I tried to sit up. Damn! "Would you like some help?" he asked, shuffling forward and crouching before me.

The word barely touched my lips before his big hand came out and cradled the back of my neck. At the contact of our skin, my mind exploded, stars danced in my visions as the warm liquid soothed my cracked lips.

"Are you always this pale, or should I be more worried?" he asked, smirking.

The question woke me from the trance I had found myself in. The first attempt to speak was interrupted by a noise I'd rather forget about. Clearing my throat, I tried again, a small gruffly sound escaping.

"They call me Ghost," I said.

His head fell to the side, his long black braid swinging wildly, looking at me with a weird expression on his face.

"You don't like it, do you?" I tried to shake my head, but instantly regretted it as it started throbbing intensely. Instead, I tried to form my lips into saying no, but I could still barely speak.

"You do not need to speak; I can hear you just fine. The fire is almost ready, do you eat?" He asked, no hint of amusement in such a strange question. Do I eat?

"You are so small, forgive the insult. Are you warm enough?" he asked, probing my exhausted mind with more questions. I'm sure I should be more concerned that he can read my thoughts, especially since I was just ogling him too.

The smirk that grew on his face told me everything that I needed to know, I was like a rabbit caught in a wolf trap, he drew all my attention to him. The way he talks is so different, not particularly his language, just the way in which he uses it. As though this was the first time he had ever spoken to someone.

Between the fire and my pain, I had allowed my mind to drift in and out of consciousness, not fully relaxing though. My thoughts were not even safe around this man, so trust was not going to be easy.

I watched him sitting in front of the fire, comfortable and becoming one with the flame as it bounced off his slick abs. I'm not sure how he wasn't freezing to death, it was chilly up on top of these mountains. Whatever he was cooking smelled divine, he suddenly turned towards me as if he knew I was watching him.

"I see you are awake. Good. Dinner is served my lady," he said grinning and pushed forward the sweet-smelling meat. Root vegetables and some sticky berry sauce was also on the plate. How long had I spaced out for? When did he have time to cook all of this? I attempted to push myself up once again, my arms still failing me, I felt something rough against my hands, pulling it out from underneath me I realised it was just one of many branches I was laid up on. I could not feel it under my actual body, as it was still numb.

"Here."

Warm hands once again found themselves upon my body, tucking under my armpits and gently lifting me up. He moved me with ease, like throwing around a bag of cotton. "Is this ok?" he asked.

He used his knees to prop my body up, heat burst through me, my body craving the fire that his skin provided. I had finally managed to relax, but my hands still shook as I reached for the plate. "Thank you," I whispered, before inhaling the food in the most unladylike way I possibly could. But at this point I didn't care, I nearly died today, and I was hungry. Plus, this man I didn't know and apparently had a habit of reading people's thoughts was now sitting cross legged behind me consuming the same meal he prepared for me as he slowly nursed me back to health.

Could this day get any –

"Fester!"

"No, it's Emmet actually."

I rolled my eyes before realising what he said. Emmet? Wasn't that the name that the voices had whispered to me in the lake? What the hell is happening here?

As if he sensed my internal war, and my thoughts, he quickly moved. My back suddenly grew cold, and I stretched out my arms quickly to try and hold my weight.

"I can see the gears in your mind turning, and I know you're about to piece two and two together. So, if you want me to leave, or you would like me to take you back to the village, I will. But, if you would like some answers – or you're just curious to see beyond what you thought was possible, then I would be happy to answer them for you," he said, but the look in his devilishly red eyes is what prompted me to stay rooted to the spot. His left eye watched me, full of sorrow and pleading with me to stay. Whereas his right eye blazed full of anger and danced like a living flame.

Like magic the puzzle pieces slotted perfectly together in my mind, I took in my surroundings, observing the mountain range that this man had chosen for his habitat. The pile of animal bones that I spotted off to the side, hidden in the shadows.

"Do you know, or are you..."

"I am Emmet, although to your people I am known by a different name. I want you to know that you are not in any danger," he sighed, folding his legs under him.

I couldn't run even if I wanted to, I was just too curious. But I could just imagine how frantic Fester would be by now. There would be hell to pay when I returned, if I returned.

"Just say the word, I will wrap you up in that blanket and carry you right to your home. But may I ask you one question? Will you please keep my secret?" He pleaded.

Again, with crazy eyes.

I can't promise something I don't even know about, if you are about to tell me... the thing I'm thinking... then you have no idea what that means to me. I did not have to say any of that out loud, he could hear me say it in my mind.

"I understand. I will give you time to consider it. The Dark One... is a part of me. A curse that was bestowed upon me as a newborn. His flame runs through my veins but unfortunately, I can't control him. I don't know why your village entices him, nor do I know why I am trapped on this island. Neither do I know how I got here. The earliest memory I have is opening my eyes to this mountainside, with a piece of paper that said my name, and my age. Five."

Five? That can't be right. I shuffled, my arms growing stiff and aching as much as my nearly broken mind.

"May I?" he asked, holding out his arms.

Reaching with one hand first, he shuffled forward and wrapped his arms around my frail frame, slowly moving me back to the floor.

The wind shifted, swirling the smoke from the fire, high into the air. This mountainside must be well protected, as we have never seen smoke coming from up here, probably a good thing really considering a dragon who spits fire lives up here. Emmet snorted, listening to the thoughts in my head , maybe I'm funny? No, impossible, he just wants to stay in my good books. "I have no intentions of purely flattering you, I have been alone my entire life, why would I need to lie and manipulate," he said, setting my head down gently and positioning my body comfortably against the soft earth.

I could feel the hot tears pricking the corners of my eyes. "You have been alone?" I whispered.

I didn't need to see the nod of his head, the flash of emotions across his deep eyes was enough. Listening to his story, I had so many emotions swirling around my mind, touching my heart and soul. We had it all wrong, not only have the village Elders been lying to us but we don't even know the half of what has been happening.

Poor Emmet had been left to deal with it all, alone, his whole life. I couldn't imagine a worse fate. Here I was, thinking that the worst thing to happen was the dragon ripping my father from my life, dragging his body away, mercilessly. That's how I had discovered charcoal in the fir – "He what?"

His face had paled, breath emptied from his lungs as he drew his knees into him, making himself into the smallest shape he possibly could.

"I am so sorry Elle; I had no idea. Goodness, what must you think of me."

"Funny thing is, I came all the way here to find the dragon and kill him." I stated.

He looked up in alarm.

"But as it turns out, I did not find a dragon, I found a man who just wishes not to be cursed by this beast. He not only violates us, but also you, by making you do unspeakable things."

I watched as he rubbed his broad hands up and down his tan arms, I'm not sure why it took me so long to even realise. Through the smoke, I could see his whole outline, the long curves and the jagged marks that depict the war between his human skin and the dragon that demands to be released. Who did this to him?

His head suddenly shot up, listening to my internal monologue. "No, not the marks, I didn't mean those. Who was it that cursed you, and left you alone as a child?"

He only shook his head, emphasising that he did not know who or why.

"I'm cold," I whispered.

His answers were very few, but of what I did know, I would be keeping a secret. Hope was the only thing between us, like a silvery thread of starlight. But all the same, everything was a lot to take in.

I started this mission with high spirits that I would catch this dragon, and I would avenge my father. But now that I am here, and I know part of the truth, I realise I can no longer do that. Not only did the human cursed to be the dragon save me, but he is also a very kind person.

"You think I'm kind?"

Amusement lit his face, his little smirk returning to that handsome face of his. If it wasn't for the fact he had saved me, and nourished me back to health, I may have punched that smirk off his face, but I'll be nice.

I'd have to return to my village soon, my mum and Fester would be getting worried by now. I would have to concoct some kind of story that was believable, but as soon as everything calmed down again and Fester wasn't being his overprotective self like I knew he would be, then I was going to come back out here and explore.

Try to find some answers for Emmet, work out who cursed him and why.

Emmet gave me a look of wonder, "Why would you help me? After everything the dragon has done to you?"

Don't look at me like that. You are not the dragon so I will help you, once I am able to lift my body off the floor with ease then we will start to hunt together. But first my family needs to know that I am okay – I thought.

"But I_" He began, not bothering to continue when I scowled at him.

As the saying goes, in the blink of an eye, he was gone. It was like magic, one minute he was there the next he was not. Suddenly I felt his hot hands all over my body, picking me up like I was a sack of potatoes, to be honest

I felt more like jelly. I was just grateful that my hair was no longer tickling my neck and hard as a rock laid underneath me, that hurt.

"Well, now you know not to swim in the lake," he chuckled.

"You know, for someone who has been alone for his entire life, you are surprisingly well... normal?" I cringed at the word.

I felt the rumble first before I heard him laugh, he had drawn me closer to his chest as he began the journey towards my home.

"You should probably put on a shirt," I mumbled.

He winked. That's when my stomach decided to flutter.

Chapter 6

Most of the journey home was silent.

We had the occasional question coming into the conversation, but besides that the silence between us felt comfortable. My bare skin touching his, made me erupt in fire and starlight. My eyes met his, and I got lost in them, I felt like I was floating in mid-air. Was this some kind of magic? Was he casting a spell on me? With my sheltered life, I didn't know what was out here past the village. I didn't know anything about the island, the history of our village or even the Dark One himself. Explanations are needed, what have we been fighting for and against? And why? But I'm worried that they don't even know either.

Walking out of the woods back into my village, the first thing that came into view is a pacing and furious Fester. We had prepared for this on the way here, created an appropriate story that would cover us both, making sure no one could be suspicious. But I knew Fester, he probably would still be suspicious.

"You can do this."

Emmet's gentle whisper sent a shiver down the back of my neck, every hair standing to attention as his lip brushed the outer edge of my ear. It took all of three seconds for good old 'Ter bear to realise I was there, then he came racing over, embracing me in a bear hug. Practically snatching me out of Emmet's arms.

"What the hell happened to you!" Fester demanded.

I knew it was directed at me, but he also looked at Emmet waiting for one of us to answer. I had to rely on Emmet to speak for us, my body, voice and my spirit was still taking an internal beating from the lake's invasion.

"I found her in the lake, I managed to warm her up and now I am bringing her home. Elle kept saying she was strong enough to travel but I know she needs time to heal. So, I promised I would bring her back to her mother," Emmet insisted.

He promised he wouldn't leave, not until we had planned on how to find answers. Plus, we have a spare room, so he could just stay there. But that also depends on if everyone can stay in control of their emotions.

"Hello little Ghost," Fester sighed, resting his forehead on mine.

The warmth of his skin used to make me feel alive, now it felt wrong. My eyes turned to find Emmet's. Sometimes I really wish I could hear what he was thinking too. His small smile that looked somewhat like sadness and a smirk at the same time, told me that he really wished I could too.

"Elle!" Mum shouted, rushing to my side.

After a quick explanation (with a few white lies), she guided us into my room, where Fester set me down upon the bed. Emmet gently pushed forward into the room, walking in between my absentminded mother and a glowering Fester.

Bending down, he gently lifted my head with one of his hands and undid my braid with the other.

"She hates to lay on it," he said with a wink, before stepping back and standing against the wall.

Fester looked ready to fight, but thankfully sleep called out to me and this time I could not refuse her.

My aching bones, and broken dreams woke me up just as the sun was rising. I had slept for a long time, but it had been interrupted, visions of half conversations and blurry faces kept calling out to me as my brain tried to reset.

As my eyes adjusted to the light in the room, I was not surprised to see Fester spread out on the floor beside my bed.

"Hey 'Ter bear," I said, voice croaking but sounding more human than before.

Good morning to you too Emmet, wherever you are, as I know you can hear me. You boys took good care of me whilst I slept, oh how the girls in the village would be so jealous seeing you two specimens escorting me around.

Knowing he was going to charge in here and demand I stay in bed another day, I quickly shot a warning through my thoughts to him that my legs and spine were protesting, so regardless of his attempts to stop me it would be futile.

"You look better, do you feel better?" Fester asked, brushing the hair from his eyes and coming to sit on the bed with me. I sighed deeply, trying not to cringe at the uncomfortable pain in my chest. That lake really was a nasty piece of work.

"Emmet is asleep in the next room. He tried to explain everything to us last night, but a few things just aren't adding up. Plus, I want to be furious with you but at the same time I can't because I'm just so happy that you are okay." His forehead, once again, fell against mine, his breath fanning across my face. I used to live for moments like this, the closeness and intimacy that he provided. But now it just feels wrong. The tune in my heart now played for someone else, someone different and unique, a new kind of love. Only one name came to my mind.

Even the thought of being in love with Emmet, made all my emotions swirl and shake. I knew that he knew, no way could someone read my mind all day every day and not know. I'm just glad he never brought it up as it would cause a bucket load of awkwardness.

"What are you thinking so intently about?" Fester asked, moving mere inches from my face. "Nothing I-"

My voice was muffled by the sudden attack of Fester's lips. They moved hurriedly, roughly against my own as I tried to close them. I put every will, every strand of strength I had into my arms to raise them, to try to push him away but I couldn't. Whining in the back of my throat, insisting that this is not what I wanted, only seemed to egg him on. I suddenly caught a break, gulping in air as he pulled back gasping for only a moment.

Before he could continue, I managed to turn my head away, figuring out the first word I could in the hopes he would stop.

"No."

"What," he said.

He didn't move, my eyes met him, and I tried to be kind.

"No," I whispered.

"But…I love you?" he said.

My heart began to ache, for so long I wanted to hear those words, but now I didn't.

"I'm sorry," I said, hot liquid splashing down my face, as my tears leaked from my eyes.

Time seemed to pause for him, his head slowly moving side to side, his eyes never leaving mine. Unblinking and unnerving. "No…" he whispered.

As he moved forward, I waited for his forehead to meet mine, praying that he understood. My eyes fluttered closed as relief spread through me. Quickly, shattering as once again his lips desperately moved against mine.

His fumbling fingers started searching beneath the safety of my blanket as pure panic froze my heart in fear. I can't do anything. Even if my limbs permitted me movement, Fester was so much stronger than I was. Unyielding rage and need for control seeped out of every single one of his pores, my nose filling with the heat of it. His breath had turned sour as he forced his tongue past the barrier of my lips.

Sobbing, I willed my mind to reach out to the only person that I knew could save me. I'm sorry that I had to.

Suddenly, Fester flew off me. Hitting the floor as Emmet bent down to make sure I was okay. He didn't try to touch me, only scanned my face and grew angrier at the sight of my tears.

His teeth ground together, his braid whipping round quickly as he stood over Fester's crumpled body.

You must calm down Emmet, I thought, we cannot risk you waking the dragon.

"He hurt you."

I know he must have made a mistake; Fester would never want to hurt me... I'm sure of it. Please, don't hurt him. Emmet picked him up, Fetser's eyes widened as he looked between the both of us.

I watched through glazed eyes as he sat him roughly in the chair outside my room and then stalked outside.

He reappeared outside my window, pacing and protecting. The look in those red eyes told me this wasn't over. Or maybe, it was the smoke emitting from Emmet's nose. Or even the fact Fester had just kicked the chair over and is now running outside.

Quick, I need to do something!

Emmet expected his advance and blocked him, but the force knocked them both to the ground. Listening to the shuffling and groaning, I tried to sit up on my own. I could see a few familiar faces appear through the window, they slowly edged towards the fight.

"How dare you!" Fester spat, finding his feet.

"How dare I? How dare you. She's lying there half dead, and you think it's ok to go after what you want. SHE TOLD YOU NO!" His face darkened, and I watched as the hand he braced against the windowsill suddenly grew claws.

"She's mine! I have loved her since the day we met. It's going to happen eventually, she just needed a little push in the right direction," Fester said, raising his fists towards Emmet.

I know he must feel hurt, he knew the minute I came home that he no longer had any hold in my life. If he thinks that I don't feel awful about it, then he's frankly quite mistaken and doesn't know me very well at all.

Seeing him this way was frightening. I felt like I didn't know him at all, this person in front of me was a stranger.

As more intolerable words were exchanged, Mum suddenly ran into my room. She had spent all night fashioning a long sturdy cane for me to lean on, with a beautiful rose carved into the top. If my father was here right now, he would be so proud.

Fester's father would box his ears if he could see the way his son was behaving.

With the help of my mum and my new cane, I hobbled outside, the crowd parted as I struggled through.

"Please, just stop," I croaked, my voice barely heard over the autumn breeze.

My muscles ached, the tears flowed freely from eyes once more, as I took control of the cane and situated myself between them. Fester immediately tried to grab me, my waist mere inches away from his hands once again, that's when we all heard the dragon's cry.

The last thing I saw was Emmet's eyes as the smoke washed away his human form and recreated him in the flame. The beast was here once again, changed by anger and fear as his human form tried to protect me. This was all my fault; his secret is out all because of me. My feet scraped against rock as Fester suddenly hooked me up under my armpits and dragged my body back.

"GET OFF ME!"

Suddenly, the scream ripped from me, drawing the Dark Ones' attention, this put us in immediate danger. My voice was spent, I swung my cane at Fester's head, making just enough contact for him to drop me to the ground. I crumpled at his feet like a sack of potatoes, as my ankle couldn't hold my weight. The dragon stalked towards us, on one side I watched people run away in horror but on the other side I watched the warriors collect their weapons and take aim.

I watched Fester come into view, watched as the truth dawned on him, and for a moment I felt ashamed. For a split second, I wondered if Emmet had some kind of magical claim over my mind and somehow had tricked me into thinking and feeling all those things I had. Then I watched Fester reach for his sword. He ordered everyone else to stand down as he approached the Dark One, entering the battle.

My thoughts were no longer negative, I knew there was no spell tricking me into my feelings for Emmet, like something had just clicked. A raw, ancient energy seeped into my bones, strengthening every part of me. I tried to yell, my voice still unheard and broken. Yet each step I took became easier, until I found myself standing in front of the one I loved and the one I used to love.

"No," I said firmly, my voice breaking his unruly focus.

"Get out of the way Elle. I don't want you to get hurt."

"I'm already hurt, Fester. You hurt me," I said as my lip trembled, and he lowered his sword.

"And all for what! This monster lied to you too," he shouted.

"No, he didn't. I've known since the moment he saved my life."

His face changed to one of disbelief. "So, you lied to us. You brought the monster that has ripped our families apart to our homes and put us in danger?"

My mind and heart pleaded with my once best friend, trying to get him to understand why. But Fester once again raised his sword, but this time it was at me; I closed my eyes waiting for the impact. Someone screamed, and I found myself high in the sky as the great beast carried me home to his nest.

Chapter 7

The dragon placed me gently on the earth and stalked away. One wary eye watched me as it tucked itself into its wings and curled its tail. Huffing once before finally relaxing, amber smoke began to swirl once again. Two red eyes shone through, then his knees hit the soil below him. I crawled over to him.

"Emmet," I called, putting my hand out, as I entered the shield of smoke.

It tickled my throat and warmed the first layer of my skin. Warm hands enveloped me, placing me on my knees in front of him. Part of my body recoiled, but I needed his help.

"I'm so sorry," he gulped, and I noticed the glistening wetness from his tears down his cheeks.

With a tentative glance, I wrapped my arms around his shoulders, and he hugged me back so gently. Taking a moment to breathe him in, a beautiful concoction of musk and sweet fruits. Like orange or some other citrus. I could see scars upon his skin, they told a million stories.

"The night I did this to myself, the dragon allowed me to look through his eyes for only a moment. We flew high in the sky, and I felt as though I could reach out a wing and touch the moon. He raised his strong snout towards the stars, inhaling, then locked me back inside my mind. I have carried that scent with me every day, and then I met you."

I watched his face as he spoke to me, and saw so many different emotions flicker across his features.

"I instantly knew you were special, not just because I found you still alive after enduring the lake. But because your presence makes me feel how that moment did. Like the peace that the night sky brings."

An onslaught of emotions overwhelmed my mind and body, from almost dying at the lake till now, it was too much for me to contain. I screamed internally, as the tears slid down my face.

"Do not blame yourself for his dishonourable actions. Only he can be at fault, you were very clear with him. What he did is not ok, but if you want to go back, I will take you there. All you need to do is ask." He stated.

"I will go back, but not right now. How about we build a fire, let's get warm whilst I navigate my mixed feelings just for a little bit."

My heart was beating wildly, my chest fighting to take a deep inhale. Emmet slowly rose to his feet leaving me sat on the floor, without another word he started to gather the kindling.

Within minutes, he had enough wood to keep a new fire going for hours.

My eyes moved with the flames, watching them flicker and dance, hypnotising me in a way. Heat radiated my front from the fire and from the side as Emmet occupied the space beside me, his body heat made me feel safe, like it was enveloping me in a hug.

I must've fallen asleep at some point because when I woke up, I was back in my own room laid on my bed, with my hair brushed over the back of my pillow so I would be comfortable. Emmet must've snuck me back in. As confusing as that thought was, I needed to check on my mother. She must be worried after everything that happened yesterday. As I pushed myself up, a single piece of my sketchbook paper floated to the ground. I reached out a hand for it, grimacing from the pain.

'I want it to be your choice, you know where I am if you need me. All my heart, E.'

My chest ached, the air around me suddenly thick and stuffy. My whole being called out to him, it was as if we were connected by a silvery thread of starlight that was slowly fading now that we were apart. Scanning my room, I found the cane resting against the bottom of my bed. It was a little burnt, but it still worked as I lent everything I had against it.

With a few stumbles, I found my footing and hobbled barefoot across the cold morning floor. My mother's door remained open, her wood tools stretched across the bed and materials at her feet.

She had been waiting for me, when I placed my hand on her shoulder it took her a few moments for her to register my presence. But was quick to demand what the hell was going on, I couldn't help but smile, no matter what my mother was going through she always cared about me. But I knew what I wanted to do now; I had known since I read that little piece of paper. My heart had roared to life, my love for Emmet was like a ball of fire getting bigger every moment.

Taking hold of my mother's hands, I explained to her about what had happened, and about my decision to help Emmet find the answers he has been searching for his whole life. I would forever store this moment in my heart, because although tears were involved, my mother accepted my decision. My mother knew I loved her, I always would, but this was a path I had to take. One day I would return here, to the place I called home for the longest of times, but for now I will have to miss her.

As for Fester, now he's calm, perhaps I will give him an opportunity to explain himself. Although I am pretty sure I know what he will say, and no excuse will be good enough for what he did. My heart hurt for just a moment, but I forced it to a stop. I would no longer feel pain for someone who could hurt me at my lowest.

I bid farewell to my mother, walking towards the one place I knew Fester would visit today; only to find him already perched there upon our rock. The cane sank into the sand, becoming completely useless to me as I slowly approached him. It wasn't till I was standing right in his eye line that he noticed I was there. He jumped up to try to help me, but I raised my hand motioning for him to stop in his tracks.

"No," I said, "Please sit down."

He obeyed warily.

"I will listen to what you have to say first, but please know that I have already made up my mind. Once you have finished, I will be leaving so this is your time to say goodbye."

His face looked alarmed as I said this.

"Say goodbye? What do you..." I held my hand up again as he tried to advance.

"Are you telling me you are going to be with that monster?" he asked, his voice deep with emotions that were so clearly painted on his face.

"I am not here to discuss him or my plans. Only to hear what explanation you have for what you did to me. I do not owe you my time but given our history I decided to give you a chance," I said, trying to swallow the pit forming in my throat. "I love you little Ghost."

"Is that it? Is that really your entire explanation?" I asked, my legs growing tired as my whole body weighed down upon them.

"No and yes. I thought you felt the same way, and then you disappeared, my whole heart felt like it had shattered. Losing you and then seeing HIM carry you in his arms... it was too much," he explained.

"So that gave you the right to do what you did?"

"I don't... is that all you have to say to me? Really, after everything we have been through you can't just see that what I did was a tiny mistake, one that I thought we could move past," he said, voice raising with every syllable.

"Maybe you can get past it, Fester, but in my eyes the second you forced yourself on to me was the moment you signed the death certificate on our friendship." I blinked hard.

"It's him saying this, putting words in your mouth. This isn't you. You would never do this to me!" He shouted, he once again tried to slowly advance towards me. I swung the cane in between us, one side hitting my own chest, the other pushing against him.

"What... Are you scared of me now Elle? You know I would never hurt you. All I have done in our entire lives is protect, love and support you. Is this really the thanks I get for it? I could've chosen anyone from this village, BUT I CHOSE YOU!" He screamed.

His face was now a shade of purple, somewhat like a blackcurrant, his fists were clenched at his sides. Part of me panicked, fearing what he would do, but it was time to leave.

"Goodbye Fester, I am leaving and maybe one day I will be back, but I am not sure. Regardless, I hope you grow into the man I always thought you could be, not this stranger that I see before me. Maybe meet someone, be happy. I will not think of you again, my thoughts of you are now tainted by the hurt you caused trying to control my life. We are over, and when life is done with, I will see you in hell," with my back straight I turned around and walked away.

I started my slow walk through the woods, the village slowly became nothing more than a scent on the wild breeze.

Chapter 8

It was like an internal navigation, the silvery thread that binds us, guided me towards him.

Past the Dead Lake and through the stone mountains, climbing higher and further until my lungs give out. My knees bent, hands atop of them as I tried to breathe air in, begging for a moment of relief. My body had taken too much trauma these past few days, I was struggling. He found me in that exact position.

"Have you come to say goodbye?" He asked, standing an arm's length away.

"Please," I said with a smirk. "You can't tease a girl with the ultimate adventure and expect her to walk away," I chuckled.

Everyone always underestimated me.

"So, you are here just for the adventure?" His question was enhanced with a hint of sadness.

"Amongst other things," I teased, taking a step closer.

"Really, like what," he said, matching my movements.

"I hear there is a great dragon that needs taming."

He growled at me, stalking closer.

"And an even greater man who deserves some company," I said, my hands snaking around his neck.

"May I touch you?" He asked, so much like a gentleman.

My smile grew, making my cheeks hurt, I nodded my approval. Gentle hands found the small of my back, pushing me closer into him, I instantly warmed internally and externally.

"May I kiss you?" I asked, the vulnerability shivered down my spine.

A small part of me delighted in his surprise, shown so easily on his face. His arms around me tightened ever so slightly. Not wasting any time, he leant down, eyes focused intently on my lips.

Every breath left my body as we finally made contact; I could see stars.

His tender touch sent me straight to heaven, our lips moulded together as if they were one. I was so lost in this feeling that I was not prepared for the onslaught of images that soon filled my mind.

They came out of nowhere, blanketed my mind like an old-fashioned film. But as quickly as they came, they went away just as fast. I then realised he had pulled his lips away, I missed the warmth of them, he left my lips tingling.

"What. Was. That?" I gasped, inhaling fresh mountain air deeply.

"Something I can only suspect as a love greater than explanation itself," he said, his voice as warm as his touch. I wanted to melt back into him.

"As much as I would love to dig deeper into all that soulmate stuff, that is not what I meant. Did you not just get that whirlwind of a message too?" I asked, drawing myself back and pacing.

I got three steps before my knee barked in pain and insisted that I give up.

"The fire isn't far, may I?"

He scooped me up, rounding the peak and tucking us safely away in the safety of the mountain.

"When you kissed me, something happened. I don't know why but I think it was some kind of message. One we should be listening to," I explained, once again finding my feet.

"Okay?"

"I need to hurry up and heal fast," I said, huffing as the irony of our situation became clear.

"Why?" he asked, his hands holding my tired frame.

"Because we need to return to the place where it all began, and for this one you may want to wear a shirt. We need to go swimming, so it may be too cold, even for you."

The fire lay between us, the flickering flame dancing wildly like the pace of my heart. I tried to make sense of the vision that unlocked when my lips had touched Emmet's.

"Maybe we should kiss again?" He teased.

My body sang as his arms wound around me, pulling me tightly against his chest. If it was even possible my heart started to beat harder. The fire around us exploded, flames licking at our skin.

The cool breeze fluttered across my cheek, travelling slowly down my neck and skipping across my spine. Emmet's hands curled around my face, drawing me even closer than humanly possible. Our lips moved together rhythmically; I craved his touch like a kid to candy. With each moment we spent together, I wished for more.

"Anything?" He mumbled against my lips, panting slightly; his damp lips glowing in the moonlight. Nothing. I spent a long time today trying to piece together the fragments that I could remember. Pulling and pushing pieces in every direction, only to come out with the same image every time. The jagged edge entices me, promising more answers if I just trust it and take the first plunge.

Quite hilarious considering how dangerous the plunge was last time.

I was intrigued as to why the lake called for Emmet by name, like they were old friends. But I know now that I should proceed with caution. One more night's sleep and we shall start our journey to find answers.

"I still hate this idea," Emmet muttered.

His long legs stretched out in front of him, his hands relaxing into the earth.

"I know. Me too but it is the only lead we have got. What if –"

"Nope."

"But –"

"Nu uh."

"Will you just let me —"

"The biggest, longest, fattest nope in the whole world," he sang, leaning forward to poke around at the fire.

"It could be the only way to know," I said.

"If this is the path you want to take, then we will go together or not at all."

I did not miss the look in his eyes, I placed the palm of my hand lightly on his lower back.

Smoke rose swiftly into the sky, offering us a dance before drifting away. "I'm scared."

"Me too."

Sleep would not be our friend tonight. We tossed and turned, backs to each other for heat. But that silvery thread that guided us together, remained between us.

The soft moss provided the perfect barrier for our bodies, stopping us from touching the hard ground below.

Time soon passed, bringing with it more questions than we already had. Not to mention, a god-awful headache from the lack of sleep. At the first break of the day, I found my strength.

"Are you ready?"

A warm steady hand met the small of my back, sparks floated up my spine, a sense of paralysis washed over me for just a second.

Emmet's mischievous grin came into view, the smile didn't quite reach his eyes though, those red orbs swirled with worry. Is his mind ever still? His face fell, answering my question. Apparently, I don't need to be able to read his thoughts to know him. Maybe it's a mate thing – oh god. I don't know anything about that sort of thing. I haven't got time to think about that right now. We need to get the dragon away from the village and Emmet and I need to get away from Fester. Part of my mind wondered if I would see him again, but the other didn't know if I wanted to.

With that thought alone, another sliver of my heart broke. For someone nicknamed Ghost, I hold a lot of soul.

"You have the most beautiful soul of anyone I have ever met," Emmet whispered, his breath tickling my ear as he embraced me one last time. I wanted to mention that he hadn't met many other people, but it was the sentiment that counted.

This was to be the beginning of our very first adventure together, one that might finally provide Emmet with answers to the questions he has held on to his entire life.

As his mate or whatever I am, I want this for him. Maybe I should try and learn more about this mate business as a newcomer, I am just a clueless human.

"Even as your internal thoughts muse on, I can still see you using air quotes you know," he chuckled, our hands gripping tightly as the descent from his camp had become slippery.

"Who put that there…" I mumbled; my cheeks flamed in embarrassment as I stumbled on a ledge of dragonstone. Emmet is lucky he did not chuckle.

The lake, unfortunately, quickly came into view. The strange green waters were more still than I had ever seen them; considering the wind was whipping violently the last time I was here. Pulling my braid to and fro, like I was a toy for their amusement.

Standing near the edge of the water, we both breathed in big gasps of air.

"We go in together, we put our heads under for as long as we can, if nothing invasive or unusual happens then we pull ourselves out. Deal?"

He nodded; his red eyes intensified as he leaned forward brushing his fiery lips against my own.

Such a small gesture, but a comfort for us both as both our nerves were shot. I focused on securing my arm around his waist, my fingers bunched in the material of his clothes, as he mimicked my movements.

My whole body jolted awake. I whipped my head towards the tree line as the strangest sensation of being watched fluttered down my spine. We prepared ourselves for the freezing cold water, bending our knees and inhaling the cool morning air. On the count of three, we launched and plunged ourselves into the deep body of water below us.

Our eyes met so easily through the water – our grip remained strong. That's when the burning started, a sensation I could only describe as being touched by the sun itself. It stirred a memory within me, a part of the message burst through my line of vision.

Water bubbled around us spinning the debris towards us, the dark viridescent waters became murky. The direction shifted, pushing everything, including us towards the centre.

All at once I knew just what we needed to do. Slipping a dagger from the sheath on my thigh, I gestured to Emmet to do the same, whatever was to come next, we needed to be prepared. Thank God, I escaped the village before Fester found out I had stolen some of the weapons, I could only imagine how angry he would be right now.

I saw Emmet's eyes widen at my last thought, the red of his eyes reflecting off the water's surface. The world around us started to darken, the water's movements intensifying. If we did not move soon, we would be dragged under before we got the chance to try to escape.

Counting to three in my head, I shouted for Emmet to follow me. Fighting against the strong current, my lungs began to burn, nausea clawing its way up my throat. Emmet's nails dug into my knuckles, the water threatening to tear us apart. But it couldn't. I wouldn't allow it to. Pulling myself to him, I wrapped my legs around his waist, my every being singing at the touch. I felt his body instantly relax, before we were gripped by an invisible force and unceremoniously yanked towards the opening void.

All sound suddenly drowned out.

My skull felt like it was being shattered as a high note pierced my ear drums. As the last of my oxygen drained, I slipped into a deep sleep and let the void swallow us whole.

Chapter 9

<u>Emmet</u>

Her limp body slid gently down my own.

I don't know where we have landed, somehow, we were dragged under the water and spat out on the other side of the void. I laid Elle down in the long-frozen grass and uncovered my weapon. Immediately we were swarmed. I backed us up the furthest I could, trying to find some cover, pulling out my long sword and swishing it side to side trying to keep the enemy back. A metallic taste filled my mouth, metal meeting metal and blood oozing from a dirty swipe at my thigh. Blood moved swiftly through my veins, bubbling and filling the empty pit of my heart. Here comes trouble. Okay Dark One, slay these things but under no circumstances do you leave Elles side. Do you hear me, don't you dare abandon her!

He listened to my every word, waiting for the last word to slip through my mind before he overtook my body. The creatures surrounding us seemed completely unfazed by my transformation, instead they pushed harder, and I realised they were not here to kill but only to weaken and capture. They did not care for me. They wanted her, they could sense that she is human, which means she did not belong in this land as they were not. If the Dark One took the brunt of the attack it would leave me with enough energy to... wait a second. I could see everything, there was no strange sensation, no sleeping until the task was done. He had simply taken over my body but had left me watching from behind the glass. I wonder if he knew about this, a quick huff and flick of his tail assured me that this was on purpose. Steam flared from his nostrils, I could already feel our body was starting to change back, but the dent he had made might give us a chance to escape.

My arms were like jelly, but I scooped Elle up and searched for that interesting inner monologue that usually blessed my ears. The reigning silence was loud and unbelievably uncomfortable, she would've had so much to say about this. Probably even more ideas about where I should be running to.

The large, dark flatlands surrounding us only offered tall grass to hide in. It would only take one small crunch of my boot for our location to be given away. As the smoke cleared, they would find us gone and unless I quickly find us cover, they would be on us again like wildfire.

Looking around, I could see a small hut in the distance, holding tightly onto Elle as I walked over to it. Managing to get in through the door before unconsciousness took over my body.

<u>Elle</u>

I fought to peel my eyes open, taking in my surroundings, I already knew where I was. Which means I already knew who I would be facing.

If I had told Emmet this is what was going to happen, he never would have agreed to come here. He will awaken soon to find me long gone, and the lonely hut he thought was safe now surrounded by palace guards ready to escort him.

My ankle grazed along the old metal, leaving a trail of dirty orange against my even paler skin. In the Forsaken Realm, humans are completely in the Queen's control; their magic directly linked across the lands that they rule. Shifting carefully, I looked down to the ground where she stood, with her feline features and bright red blood eyes. Her black lips turned upwards in a menacing grin, she had caught me and now here I am enslaved by chains.

It wouldn't be long before Emmet was brought here, he would bear witness to me hanging like a trapped bird in a cage. I surveyed the room trying to get an understanding of what we are up against, as the message from before had only shown me so much of what was to come. The rest of the message was still waiting to be deciphered, but I was unsure on how to do that.

I couldn't understand why I, an insignificant human, had been left with this impossible task. The dark marble floor below shimmered like diamonds, something inside me could detect danger though, so I know I should never let my skin touch it.

A heartbeat later and the huge doors slammed open. Shuffling feet announced Emmet's arrival. "Get your…" he yelled, his voice echoing around the large space. A small part of me had held on to that childlike hope, of him not being caught, but alas he was here.

I was hoping when the next part of the vision unlocked it would include us being freed and allowed to return home with all our answers, but somehow, I knew this was wishful thinking.

Emmet's body lurched, hitting the floor but he didn't seem to notice as his head whipped around. I knew he was looking for me. Our bond and his ability to read my thoughts allowed his eyes to instantly connect with mine. Worry rimmed those stunning eyes, and that's where his problem lies. He wears all of his emotions on his face, plain as day.

The scratch of material against the galactic marble floor drew his attention away from me and on to the Red Woman. She stopped walking just short of Emmet, tapping her toes lightly. Towering over him, heels higher than any I've ever known, she raised a finger and commanded he rise. The instruction was more threatening than any words she could have used.

Their eyes met, red on red, and I wondered if Emmet had pieced it together yet.

"Welcome home son."

Emmet

Son.

Guess we can cross that question off the list.

The woman chuckled, a harsh unkind sound.

"I knew one day you would return. And what a joyous day it is... Come," she said, spinning delicately on one heel and striding towards the large table. Elle's eyes bore into me, her thoughts racing and unclear. A faint pain loitered in my right collarbone, a familiar erratic beat. Somehow, they had sensed our presence, and somehow Elle knew.

This premonition of hers is becoming a real pain.

Her cage suddenly swung violently, a hazy web spun between her and the Red Woman's lazy finger.

"Let Elle go," I shouted, clamping my jaw as the guards threw me to the icy ground once more.

"Oh, your little girlfriend… sure. But you should know, the minute a human's feet touch this marble floor they burn from the inside out." She laughed, her face tight.

I couldn't risk Elle's life, but how the hell were we going to get out of here now.

"Surely, you'll let her go for me. I'm your son."

Desperation leaked through my voice, I could practically hear the Dark One roll his eyes at my pitiful attempt of negotiation.

"Please. You were my son for all of five minutes before that disappointment sent you away. Speaking of which, shall we go and see dear old dad," she snapped, jabbing a long black menacing nail towards Elle. Elle suddenly disappeared. Blood pounded in my ears.

I got up and walked around the corner following the woman who calls me son, the cold stone met my bare feet, slapping hard with each step. It grounded me.

We ventured down endless stairs, stone melted into jagged rock. Green hues danced in the corners of my eyes. Water dripped thickly down the walls, melting into the sound of our echoing footsteps. My nose stung and watered as a strong, damp, putrid scent clung to my skin. Poor Elle. The Red Woman paced gracefully down, leading the way into a large shadowy room. Facing us stood two large cells, they were larger than Elle's hut back home. In one of them was Elle.

I slipped on the rock as I ran over, wincing as a sharp point jabbed right into the balls of my feet.

"Emmet, are you hurt?" She asked, her eyes shining, the glint of tears in her eyes.

"You're worried about me?" I chuckled, reaching for her hand.

"Yes yes, very touching. Don't forget about your father, son."

Triumph edged her ice-cold voice, as someone approached from the shadowy corner in the other cell. Human, this man is utterly human. Made from paper skin and brittle bones. With grey hair down to his knees and enough wrinkles that I could count the years he has been trapped in this cell. I took him in, observed his home and almost wept as his husky voice stirred an ancient feeling in my chest. "Emari?"

Elle

Watching the interaction was nothing compared to feeling it.

I would give anything to see my father again. The warrior in me knows that death is a part of life, no matter how swift. But even just a chance to say goodbye, to feel his strong arms around me, or even hear his ankles crack when he rolled out of bed in the mornings. To know that Emmet is getting that experience and more right now... It feels like a blessing. Their hands embraced. The cold bars stung under my fingers, my skin already bruising. At least I'll finally have some colour to me.

"This is Elle, she is my mate," he said, joy bursting through me.

The air around us thinned, even the wind didn't dare move. I braced myself, watching the Red Woman's movements. I didn't know what was about to happen. The fates had decided I would not need this information, so I could not help.

"Now that is interesting," she said, emphasising every word.

Her heels clicked menacingly on the rock, even the shadows seemed to shrink away in her presence.

"But tell me dear son… Who's true mate is she? Yours, or your brothers?"

The moment my flight or fight instinct kicked in, I knew what was about to happen. I backed away from the cell door, trying to navigate Emmet's eyes from the shadows, instead I found a blazing flame. His mother's words had dragged the Dark One from his slumber. But how could he let her words affect him so easily? Even if he had a brother, he doesn't have any memory of him. The door to my cell suddenly clicked open, her slender arm beckoned me to her. My feet were deeply rooted to the damp rock.

For a moment I thought I saw the fire flame out; that was until the Red Woman's hand suddenly appeared and struck me powerfully against my pale cheek.

My neck recoiled, stiffening at the impact. Smoke choked the room as a deafening roar broke the barrier of the dungeon and brought crowds of guards to their Queens side. Whether it be fear or true loyalty, she was going to be fine. But what about the rest of us? What about Emmet? Exactly how in control of the Dark One is he.

It took no time at all for all my questions to be answered, all sense of logical thoughts slipped from my mind. As I watched the smoke clear, the Red Woman walked towards the mighty beast, the last thing I expected was for it to bend its knees and bow its great head.

Notably, his father did in fact not look shocked.

"Emmet," I whispered, edging towards the opening. The heat from his snout rippled across my skull. The Red Woman, this beast's mother, grinned. I reached out with my mind trying to find even an inch of him. Instead, I was met with a red-hot marble wall.

"Try again sweetie," she said, her voice like sweet venom.

"What?" My chest turned cold.

"That is not just some sweet human nickname his father gave him."

Just like that the smoke disappeared, leaving a limp and heavy Emmet sprawled along the floor. An icy feeling in my mind.

We found each other and I aided him.

"You may release the old one," his mother spat before trailing back up the staircase. She ventured off into the shadows, so we took our cue to follow. Not to mention, the sharp kick in the shins. Heaviness filled me, I tried not to let it show, only concentrating on Emmet. Making sure my mind did not wander was a hard feat.

I wasn't sure of the outcome in this scenario. To think back to when life was just as complicated, but at least I was home. I miss home. This was supposed to be Emmet's home.

Yet, he has returned to not be greeted with love and open arms but burning hatred and yearning loyalty to a psychopath. Emmet has been through so much, the little pocket within my heart that I am trying so hard to forget keeps niggling at me to open. A lot has happened in such a short time, my head hurts from everything. A gentle tug on my elbow drew me from the loudest thoughts I have ever experienced; coming back to the present awakened my eyes to the grandest room I have ever seen. Tall pillars decorated the furthest corners, whilst long tables lined the walls. How many people was she expecting? A platter of different foods spread across every single surface as far as I could see, and none of it looked edible. Drinks of all colours and consistencies bubbled over into silver trays like potions.

Emmet squeezed my hand, and he gave me a look I can only describe as 'do not consume anything.' Another kick to our shins and we were seated at the high table centred in the room. The black wood detailed with red thorned roses perfectly matched this woman, I can't imagine living in a place like this.

So devoid of life, dark and repressed.

"Won't you eat?" She asked, spearing metal into some unknown red meat.

Juice dripped down onto the plate as she drew it to her black lips.

"I'll take some answers, from the both of you," Emmet said, resting his arms calmly on the table. A server set a glass of water down in front of everyone, before they all just simply vanished. Somehow, I feel safer with them all watching.

Emmet

With a heavy sigh I attempted to tune out Elle, focusing on my breathing. A steady in… and out. "Your mother-"

"That woman is not my mother," My teeth clamped together.

"Ok, Her Majesty did something. When you and your brother were inside her womb she paid a travelling witch to perform a union; when it became clear that you were like me she decided she needed to take action in order to keep you both here and keep you both safe."

My father's eyes darted between his mate and myself. Every single word he spoke came out long and slow, clearly even the fates got it wrong sometimes.

Sipping my water, it was all I could do not to shout. Not to allow-.

"What's his name?" I asked, filling my mouth once again with the cool liquid.

"Matias. My sweet little dragon," said the Red Woman, her face beaming.

"So, my brother, he's the dragon. That's him taking over control?"

"See son, this is why you're not the favourite," she chuckled, raising a glass of something that looked suspiciously like blood to her lips, I almost gagged as I drained the last of my water.

"But don't you worry my dear little one. The travelling witch didn't leave me without an escape clause. In fact, I'd bet the potion sets to work almost immediately."

Her eyes flickered to my water glass. Everything finally connected, I kicked back my chair not even thinking before I dragged Elle's chair to the edge of the room. My body began to vibrate. How could I have been so stupid? So easily distracted. Fire sparked up every nerve, crawling out through every pore. Falling to my knees I looked for her, knowing that for me, it wasn't a question.

Elle

Horrific. Agonising. Gut-wrenching. That was all the emotions I felt just from watching the scene before me. I could not imagine how Emmet must be feeling right now. Or I suppose it's Emari. His skin, slick with sweat, bubbled and morphed.

I covered my ears, his panting and groaning continued to get louder, his voice hoarse by the time his skin erupted in ice and flame. Then he screamed. A noise unlike anything I have ever heard before, caught between a man and a beast. His face contorted, skin stretching and eyes popping. God, I can't watch this, covering my eyes. A bony hand met my shoulder, gripping gently in a way that made me lower my hands.

"He will be ok," his father said.

Smiling up at him, I almost became unhinged as Emmet screamed again. When this is through, he should choose his own -.

Pain split across my skull, my vision darkening as once again a part of the vision unlocked. This time it brought me hope but this next part will be tricky. I wasn't sure how Emmet would feel about it, nor do I know how I feel about it.

"Elle..."

My name slipped from his lips in a painful moan before his stomach heaved and a large black mass plopped to the floor. He belched, loudly, before finally collapsing to the floor in exhaustion. We didn't dare move, waiting as the mass rippled and grew. Heat radiated from it, steam creating a thick mist in the air. I didn't miss seeing the

Red Woman move whilst pulling out a small vial, three drops of whatever was within touched the forming mass with a hiss. Like a ripple effect, the black scales melted together and began his transformation from beast to man. With a last wet pop, he was here. His brother lay next to him, identical in all but one feature.

With a deep breath they pulled themselves to their knees, facing each other for the first time. Red eyes met ones of deep blue, his father's eyes. A reminder that no matter what skin you wear, beast or man the potential for either still lies within you. They watched as I hesitantly walked over to them, dropping to my knees without a single word to offer them myself, I reached for their hands.

Likewise, I reached out with my heart feeling for that silvery thread that connected our souls. On one hand I found warmth, hot fire burns passionately through this person. But the other. It called to me, like a wild breeze dancing under the stars. Matias fell away, a sad smile flashed briefly in his eyes. Just like his brother, he wore his emotions on his face. Emmet's chuckle told me everything that I needed to know.

He was my soulmate, my truest love. But above all he was my best friend. Now we had an extremely dangerous task to complete.

Chapter 11

Emmet

I saw the plan as it unfolded in her mind, a bit too easily. Should I be more concerned? She giggled, and the look of surprise that lit her beautiful face is one I will never forget. Elle, can you hear me?

Her small nod filled my heart with pure joy. Even so, it drained the last of my already depleted energy. The Red Woman finally approached, beelining for my brother.

"Welcome home son," she said, offering her manicured hand.

His body heaved, equally as exhausted from the transformation as I, he graciously accepted her hand

and even her light embrace. If she favoured her other son, why did she even bother with me?

"Come, eat. This food will not harm you."

"Thank you," he said, gladly sitting down.

Elle's small hands found me, my balance still unstable as I tried to find my feet.

"You can leave," Her Majesty commanded, waving a hand.

The big doors opened heavily with a long slow creak. I opened my mouth attempting to respond, but Elle took control. "No thanks," she said and started picking at a piece of fluff on her shirt,

The Red Woman was on her feet instantly, gone was the grace as she stomped over in her heels.

"I have what I wanted," she spat, her words aimed at me. Her face only a mere inch away from Elles, but she stood there unbothered. No, that wonderful woman just smiled.

"Leave my realm, you vile little human before I melt you down and feed you to my dragon."

"I rather think he'd like that," Elle winked at Matias.

"Have it your way," she muttered, her palms outstretched as a flame sparked and grew. Her eyes seemed to shine, a menacing grin spreading across her thin lips. Suddenly Matias sprung forward, grabbing the Red Woman and locking her hands behind her back.

Elle

Emmet and I sprung into action.

Drawing the sword from the knight's armour that stood nearby, I waited until Emmet joined his brother and disabled the Red Woman.

"What do you think you are doing?" She hissed, struggling against the hold. Her heels slipped on the smooth stone floor, but it was their father who answered.

"It's time your reign came to an end, Isla, my love." The years had weighed on him heavily.

Even through everything he had endured at the hands of the one he was fated to, you could still see the love he had for her.

Fate traps you when it sentences you to the bond.

Some flourish, some survive, whilst others must merely endure it, a blessing or a curse. "Are you ready?" I asked.

The warrior within me took over, folding away my nausea and focusing on the task at hand.

Isla started to laugh uncontrollably, it was a cold and terrifying thing.

"You really thought it would be that easy?"

Guards poured into the room, yet they didn't raise their weapons. Emmet and Matias are weak, there is only so much they could do.

"I'll make you a deal," she drawled. "Release me and I shall take you to a portal that will bring you home.

Except for you of course my dragon, we have some catching up to do."

Little did she know, this was exactly what I was waiting for her to say. Otherwise, we never would have trusted her. We would never willingly walk into such an obvious trap. We had to play the part, she could not be so easily killed there was something else we had to get first.

"Release her Emmet. I want to go home," I demanded. Begging in my head for him to play along.

"But Elle-"

"Do as your little girlfriend tells you son, I may not be so generous for much longer," she said, her smile cold. He nodded, both stepping back. Isla rolled her shoulders.

"Now then… follow me," she muttered, playing her part well.

In single file with guards following closely behind, she led us into the grand entrance to her magnificent castle. I tried my best not to trip as she led us up a steep staircase. My thighs barked and my back ached, but I always kept my focus on her, the stairs led to a large open space, multiple doors faced us, tightly shut.

"This way."

I noted the details on the oakwood doors, some with animals and others with symbols I didn't recognise.

As we came to a corner, I found my attention grabbed, my heart beginning to race. A large door with a silver knob patterned with symbols seemed to glow in my presence, every hair on my body stood to attention. Electricity sparked through the air. Anger flooded me as rough hands pulled me from the doorway and pushed me down the hallway. Emmet watched me, his face fierce at the creature handling me. The hallway narrowed, even Matias's steps faltered as he remembered where we were heading. He needed to act now.

Matias

Being linked to my brother's mind is... frustrating. He feels so many things, all at once. Plus, he never stops thinking about Elle. Which sucks, as I miss her. I knew we were never meant to be, and just like my brother when I was in control, I was not aware when he was in control. But when she was around, I somehow always knew. Still, I wish them well. Catching her eye, she gave me a nod. It's time. Isla, or my mother I should say, kept me annoyingly close as she walked, her annoying heels clicking away as she went, her gown scraping heavily along the floor. Perfect opportunity for me to just push her over, so I did.

She fell lighter than I expected, recovering far too quickly for my liking. Instantly I was detained.

"Fine then, you insolent boy. You can reside here, stuck with the ridiculous humans!" She yelled, pushing open a door and moving aside.

The creatures poked the ends of their swords into our backs, ushering us forward with earnestness. Heat radiated from the wounds, blood rising to the small incisions. We stumbled across the threshold and into the dark room, the door slammed shut behind us. It echoed through the cavernous room that bore nothing but a small window which was unlatched.

"This is a very special room, the door is sealed with magic that only I can control. Now my son, when you learn to behave yourself, I will let you out. As for your friends, well, there is only one way for them to escape," her chuckle continued all the way back down the hall. As it was foretold, she had left us all alone to die.

Chapter 12

__Elle__

Three small cots suddenly appeared, along with a bucket that I wouldn't dare touch. Well at least we were not expected to sleep on the floor, that's always a positive.

"What now?" Matias asked, stalking over to the window.

It was small enough that it made the room dark and miserable from the minimum light coming through, but also just big enough that if you wanted to throw yourself out of it you could. "We rest, then we plan," I answered.

Simple right? This time we will have to figure it out for ourselves, the premonitions can't be the only thing we get answers from.

"Actually, whilst we're asking questions, I have a few for you."

Matias settled into a cot with a sigh.

"This situation is... puzzling. Technically, we don't know you. So, what's up with the whole dragon situation?" I asked, wondering whether this is really the right time to be bringing up such trivial things.

"This is my true human form, I lost it when Emari and I joined. I am the dragon, but the dragon is not me. There is only so much control and consciousness I am open to. He is very much still a beast, with predator instincts. I'm so sorry Elle, I know what he took from you, I wish that I could've stopped it but I was merely a passenger watching through his eyes with no control. I wish I could give him back."

"Let's stick to calling him Emmet, shall we?" I said.

I wasn't sure if it was my overwhelming emotions, or the look in his eyes that drew me to him. But I wrapped my arms around his head and kissed his hair. When I stepped back, I reached for Emmet's hand and squeezed gently.

"You know, I didn't realise it until now, but I felt you there all the time. Now there is an empty space inside of me. Did you know? Emmet asked, his questions running through his head like a kaleidoscope. It was nice to be able to hear him now, Matias must've been blocking the link somehow.

"I knew. I even tried to tell you a few times. However, the magic that binds us and is contained within us, was way too strong." I moved to the window, letting brother and brother sit beside each other, finally able to get some clarity on their situation.

The boys fell asleep, exhaustion had won and finally took over, dragging them into a deep, healing slumber. Laying side by side they looked like a mirror image.

Matias' hair is a shade darker, Emmet's chin is much softer. Whilst they slept, I concocted an elaborate plan. A ridiculously dangerous one at that. Isla would most likely send someone to investigate us at some point. The only thing for us to do was make her believe we were really trapped here, then wait for nightfall. I just hope the boys would be on board.

I could feel the air around me suddenly vibrating, I had felt this before so knew something was about to appear. Not even a second after that thought, a table arrived containing three glasses of water upon its surface, and three bowls of some alien looking oats. No thanks, I choose life.

The putrid smell wafted around the room, dragging the snoring beasts from their dreams. "I don't like the smell of that-"

"One bit." Matias finished with a yawn.

I chuckled, passing the glasses of water around and wondering how long it would take them to realise that I hadn't slept and had been thinking of ways to get out of here.

Nearly all the water had gone before I decided to tell them. "I have a plan."

"A completely reckless one, I take it," Emmet chuckled.

He knew me so well. They looked at me expectantly, waiting.

"Matias, how well do you think you could call on the dragon?" I asked.

He cocked his head, considering my question. His eyes glazed over before whipping his head to the window. It seemed the brothers could also speak to each other through their thoughts.

"You really are mad," he muttered.

Worry filled me, easing only when I saw his mischievous grin.

"You think you could, do it?"

"Only one way to find out, if not then let's hope I survive the fall. Although the ocean down there looks mean," he chuckled.

He wasn't kidding, even in broad daylight the water below was darker than any night I had ever witnessed. It attacked the rocks below vigorously.

"Great, then all we must do is ride a dragon? Emmet asked.

"Then sneak back into the castle that we just escaped from, to find your mother's secret room. Kill her in the process and win over all her creature things. No biggie," I shrugged.

"Right. All I ever wanted was to know if I had family, and where they were. Why I was abandoned on that mountain top. For years I searched your village, I climbed to the highest points of the mountains and searched the sea for life. Nothing. Now I find them, my dad is the coward that sent me away, but I think in his own way it was a way to save me. My brother was connected to me my whole life and my mother hates me. Now we plan to kill her." Emmet sighed, sinking back into his cot.

Finally, I laid down, reaching for Emmet's hand. I had barely felt his warm embrace before my heavy eyelids closed and my consciousness was shot out into the universe.

Matias

Listening to Elles soft snores provided comfort as I sat up alone waiting for the sun to set. Orange began streaking across the deep sky, drawing me to the window, the view was beautiful. The air had no breeze leaving it quite stuffy, but at least it wasn't cold. I hated the cold. There was only one time I had truly ever felt cold, and that was when Emmet had hurt himself. From then on, I fought harder and harder every day for control, and to guide us towards that silvery thread that beckoned to me.

Experiencing something I knew was never going to be permanent for me, but I counted every day with her as a blessing all the same. The ache of her still resided in the small pocket in my heart.

We still have a connection through my brother, and that will be enough for me. I just needed a little more time to grieve the loss. Salt sprayed high up the cliff wall, yet it still seemed so far away. If I'm not quick enough, if I don't take control of the dragon, I will not survive. I think I could make my peace with that though.

Emmet

I watched my brother as he stared out into the dying sun, I really wished I could do more to help him. To save him from his own crushing thoughts. I'm not sure any of us are safe from the dense gravity of what we must do.

The familiar squeak of the window being unlatched on the door drew me from the bed, awakening Elle from her restless nap in the process. The creatures were human in stance, but that is where any resemblance dies. The foul odour that rolls off their green scaly bodies in a mist, sticks to you like glue. Their glowing yellow eyes pierced deep into our very souls. Satisfied with what they saw, they retreated. Now it allowed us to set our plan into motion.

Chapter 13

Elle

The dark night was soon upon us, our ability to see beyond the cliff had become void.

"Okay Matias, whenever you are ready," I said, releasing him from what I hope will not be our last embrace.

"Brother... Do not drop us."

They both chuckled before Emmet seized him into a bear hug.

"I need a cool exit line," Matias muttered, looking over at the drop.

A familiar lump swelled in my throat, hot tears pushing on the barrier of my eyelashes.

Matias took both of our hands, before facing away from us as he sat upon the brick ledge.

"On the wind, or in fire and ice, we walk together." I opened my mouth, but before I could react, he let go, ducking his head he fell to his death. Now it was all on the dragon's shoulders, hopefully he would appear.

Emmet

I watched my brother offer himself up as a sacrifice, praying that the dragon would appear and save not only him but us too. He looked almost surreal, a peaceful look upon his facial features as he hurtled at a considerable speed towards the blackness below. Swifter than lightning, he disappeared beyond the sea's mist. Now we wait.

Matias

I accept whatever my fate must be.

I let the mist rinse over my body, and the wind carry me to my new home. The roaring waves came closer, please Dark One, the only family that has ever truly accepted us needs us. Time slowed, but our descent quickened, gravity promised us a quick death.

My hands reached out hoping to feel the water before my consciousness drifted away, only to feel the sweet bite of cool air on my now leathery wings.

My heart dropped, but my body soared. He came, he had saved us.

The mist parted, yielding to my great dragon form. My eyes saw clearly for the first time, we rose steadily until

Elle and Emmet came into view. The relief, joy and love on their faces filled the empty space inside me. To have someone love me finally felt like a dream come true. The great stone wall stood unguarded on the cliff face, the gardens beyond quiet too.

Okay Dark One, it's time to rock this.

We wrapped ourselves around the building, tail holding us steady as Emmet guided Elle onto our back. Even through our thick scales we could feel her warmth, I savoured it.

The heaviness grew as Emmet slotted himself behind her and their legs clamped tightly, holding on for dear life.

I motioned, trying to control the dragons' movements. But he had other ideas, finding his balance he shot straight into the air, wind whipping our hot snout. Of all the times he could want to go for a free roam, he would choose to do it now.

"Matias, what's going on?" Elle yelled, as the castle became nothing but a dot beneath us. The Dark One remained quiet, undetected, moving further away from his mother.

I know this is scary and I know that killing our own mother feels wrong, but she is a bad person and needs to be stopped. She has this entire realm under her control, she imprisoned us and wants to control us as her greatest weapon. Not only that, but she hurt our father and will not hesitate to kill us all if we escape.

Elle has been given the sight of the future. For everyone to live safely, Isla must die, we must restore the balance in this realm. We can not abandon the people we love now, we are a part of each other, I know you feel the love for them too. So, please Dark One, do what is right, then we may rest. Our internal battle for control seemed to take a lifetime, but for our passengers it was only a mere moment.

Elle

Relief flooded through me as the Dark One suddenly changed course and began circling the castle. For such a wicked Queen, she didn't guard her home very well. The outer wall protected it from the slums she ruled below, or perhaps it was the other way around. It seemed the civilians that lived in that village dare not rush that wall and those guards that circled it, but if they only knew no one and nothing lay within the wall. Now it was time to navigate a landing spot.

"There!" I called, "A balcony on the second floor."

Hearing me, the dragon dove, my braid floating above us. The balcony opened to a hallway, dark and quiet. Sliding down the dragon's body rather ungracefully I might add, I dropped to the stone and took cover.

"Matias, find somewhere to lay low. We might need an escape."

With a brief nod of his head, he disappeared into the night, leaving behind the lingering warmth of his body. Weapons in hand, we peered into the empty space, listening for any sign of life. On our tiptoes, we snuck in through the arch and looked around. One door stood at one end of the hallway, and stairs that spiralled down on the other side. Creeping towards the door, I pressed my ear to it. Signalling to Emmet, we moved away from it.

"I'm pretty sure that is where those creature guard things sleep. There was talking and snoring from within. We need to move quickly," I whispered.

The steep stairs moved snakelike with hardly enough room for one person. I stopped just short of the bottom, which I was thankful for as the door below opened to the throne room. That mystical floor was swirling and enticing to my human feet. "Here."

Emmet grabbed under my legs, holding me close to his body. I wouldn't say I was disappointed by this, he kissed my hair in response.

"Son!"

His fathers worried whisper floated down to us. His body hung limply in a cage, his eyes heavy with exhaustion.

"What are you doing in here?" He asked, his voice hoarse.

"We are looking for a hidden room, there is something in there that can stop her terrifying reign for good," Emmet replied.

Pain floated through our bond with a force that made me want to weep.

"Her treasures are below us. She showed me them once and used the moment to trap me. It requires her blood to open the room though."

"Emmet is her son, surely it should work. Where is it?" I asked.

He took a deep struggling breath, trying to find his words. A pale hand slipped shakily through the bars, pointing towards... the throne? "We will come back for you father."

Emmet moved quickly towards the back of the throne searching for a way in, a large dragon and its wings presented itself, its golden mouth open wide.

"Here, you need to do it," Emmet said, awkwardly twisting his arm and offering his hand to me. With an apologetic smile I sliced my dagger across his palm and gripped him tightly as he squeezed his fist into the beast's mouth. With a groan, the chair slid forward, the floor opening into a seemingly bottomless void.

"Why must we keep jumping into the unknown?"

Chapter 14

My eyes squeezed close as Emmet launched us both into the abyss below.

"What is that?" I asked, trying to see past the darkness.

Thick air seemed to cling to us, we landed in a low-lit room, our feet hitting the floor sharply, twinging my already bad ankle. Pins and needles snaked up my leg as I took a turn around the enclosed room.

"It's some sort of a cave," Emmet whispered, his hand finding mine.

Mismatched wooden shelves lined the walls, candles dripping over the edge and towards the stone floor.

Various colourful orbs floated above our heads emitting a frivolous energy. A round wooden table sat centered in the room.

"This is the vial of drops Isla used on Matias. Look, here's the recipe for it," I gasped, looking over the plans.

"It looks like she's been planning on our arrival," he said, moving along the last wall. The bare rock jutted out sharp and covered in moss. "What if I…"

He touched his still bleeding hand to the rock, there was a wet pop and part of the wall seemed to fold in on itself, rock scraping against the stone flooring.

 Identical boxes lined a series of shelves. Looking at a few of them, I almost dropped one in horror.

"Is that a human heart?" I gagged, closing the box.

"This just has a velvet lining, but I think the shape pressed into it matches the vial on the table," he muttered to himself, lost in his own search.

"Elle, why don't we take a step back and you try something, anything to see if you connect with any of the boxes. Otherwise, we may be searching for a very long time."

Nodding, I waited until he stepped away and closed my eyes.

All my focus drew inwards, thinking about the task at hand. We must kill this woman, we must put an end to her terrible existence. Freeing Emmet and Matias's father from his prison, allowing everyone to heal. Palms out and keeping my eyes closed, so I remained focused, I shuffled towards the shelves. My hands moved of their own accord, guided by my pure intentions. "Can you fee-"

"Shhh!"

He chuckled, the sound drowning out as my eyes snapped open. A searing heat burned my fingertips as they brushed against a box on the highest shelf. "This lock requires your blood," I said, passing it over.

I think I should probably question my abilities more, surely this wasn't normal for a human? Anyways, at the rate that we are going, weirder things are bound to happen first.

"It's another vial."

"Read the label," I said, moving closer. "Immortales Mortales – The immortal Mortal," he read.

He peered at the swirling liquid, small red flecks bubbled inside. It shimmered under the candlelight. "She's immortal, she cannot be killed. But if she were to take this?"

"Then we could go home," he said.

His hand slipped into mine.

"Now, how the hell do we get out of here.

We really should start thinking about our exit plans before we enter somewhere.

Emmet

Turns out leaving the room meant I had to cut my hand again, blood magic was my mothers favourite pastime it seems. Her sanity is proven to be insane with this set-up, who wants to continuously hurt themselves, like really? Stairs appeared up to the throne this time, thankfully we didn't have to clamber our way out, it would've been hard to do so with Elle in my arms. When the throne slid back into place, it was as if it had never moved, the dust still lay thick on the base of the throne.

"Move quickly son!" My father called.

We heard footsteps out in the hall.

"They were just here. Her Majesty has sent them to watch over you. You must go quickly!"

Running with Elle in my arms is as awkward as it gets, my heart was racing, thumping so wildly as we started up the steps. She dropped to her feet lightly, taking the lead. As we approached the balcony, we heard the unmistakable creak of the door. Hidden behind the wall, I listened to the herd of creatures slither by.

"Seriously, what the hell are those things?" I asked, turning to find Elle leaning over the balcony.

"Matias," she called.

"You do remember we are linked, right?" I chuckled.

The Dark One appeared through the trees.

"Hurry, we must return to the room."

He huffed, clearly not impressed. Grey smoke covered us as we rose high into the sky.

I had just finished stepping into the room when we heard the latch unclasp. Thinking on her feet, Elle approached covering their view of the room.

I heard Isla asking questions, her temper rising, making the air shift in the room.

Brother, how on earth are we going to get you back into the room. As if in answer, the dragon reached out his great paws. One hung over the window ledge, the other placed into my hand, it burned as he began to transform, his scales bubbled over and smoothed out. With an agonising cry, my brother pushed through, hanging on for dear life.

"What is happening?" Isla screamed. Matias floated into the room, carried by her magic.

Play along brother.

I grabbed him by the front of his shirt with my fist, "this traitor has been drilling us for information," I said, willing my face to heat with anger. With him obstructing her view, I passed him the vial.

"Not to mention I tried to steal his mate," Matias laughed, closing the small vial in his fist.

I pushed him away from me, gearing up to make a swing at him. He ducked and dropped the vial into his boot. Well done, I thought, we make quite a good team.

In response to this, Elle flew through the room and lightly held me back.

"He may be a traitor, but he is still your brother. Let him go, Emmet."

We stepped back as Isla approached Matias.

"Is this true?"

"She told me that she was confused, her feelings just as strong for me despite the bond. I had to shoot my shot," he shrugged, slipping his hands into his pockets, playing the cool villain perfectly.

"It seems you have outlived your punishment. Trust me son, you can do so much better than this wretched human. Come," she said, turning a perfect heel and slipping from the room.

Matias turned for a moment, his thoughts loud and clear.

Yes brother, now send that monster to hell.

Matias

I had thought very limited things over the years, but there was one thought I had more than the others. I was trapped inside Emmet and the Dark One, an observer in their world. But as he had forgotten our mother, I had not. My memories were not so easily erased, I remember how she was towards us from birth. Always angry, always blaming Emmet's existence for her dragon having to be locked away. Angry at the witch for deceiving her. Realistically without Emmet we wouldn't have survived too long, my temper would've got me killed.

"You must be hungry, my sweet one, sit." Her Majesty's voice grated through my ears.

"Yes mother."

The meal passed quickly, the food exactly as I remember. Tasteless, chewy and strange. I'm almost certain we are eating the very creatures that serve her so loyally.

"You have been through such an ordeal, trapped with those disgusting humans. It was necessary though, it taught you a valuable lesson," she said, draining her glass.

"Truly it was a painful experience. But nothing is worse than the years I spent trapped inside his mind."

She looked at me thoughtfully, a part of me thought she would apologise.

But alas, she did not. All she said was, "help yourself to the wine son."

Before she set down her cup and slid it over to me; my opportunity had arisen, handed to me on a silver platter.

As sweet treats were brought out, I walked to the back of the room and located the drinks trolley. Bending down I selected a clean glass from the bottom shelf, groping for the vial in my boot as I did, pouring the blood red wine into the glass. The candlelight nearby kept the glass warmed up which allowed the wine to bubble up as it made contact. I opened the vial, and poured it in, swirling the glass in my hand allowing it to mix in with the wine. I wonder if she would feel the effects of the potion before I stick my dagger into her heart or if when it pierced her heart and pain spread through her, would she be shocked? Would she even have any regrets in her last thoughts? Opting for water, I poured my glass and took a deep breath before turning round back to the table.

"She may be human, but Elle is exactly the company I may need. Besides, we need a way to punish my brother, do we not?" I smirked, putting the glass down in front of her.

"I'm sure I can make an exception. But what of your brother?" She asked, raising the glass to her lips.

"I've certainly had enough of him."

Sorry brother, I thought internally.

The distance between us made me feel so cold, I had lived with him so long, it hurt to be apart.

Trying to look as unsuspicious as possible, I watched her take a long draught of her wine, half of her glass drained in one go. My heart threatened to jump out of my chest, the room was deadly silent, I could've heard a pin drop. Waiting for any reaction to occur. I pulled the first thought from my head.

"Perhaps, we should send him back. Take Elle as our own and send him back alone, her people will think he killed her, so they may attack him."

"Send him back? Are you quite serious? He will never stay away from his mate. He would not even enter the village. No, we must move him down to the cells, he can get to know your idiot of a father. We can set up a special room for you and your... toy," she grinned, and emptied the last drop of her drink.

How long would this potion take before it works? Pulling a long dagger from my boot, I dragged my nail along the sharp edge. She watched me, quite amused.

"Or you can put an end to him," she giggled.

"How long have you been Queen?"

"Since I killed my mother. Why?" Isla sat to attention, suspicion dancing in her hellish eyes.

"Did you ever want to be anything more?" I asked, twirling the silver blade in my palm.

"I wanted control, so I took it. I wanted loyalty, so I got it."

She watched me intently.

"Yes, what are those dreadful things?" I almost gagged at the thought of them swirling around my stomach.

"Ah, those are a special breed, something of my own creation. I shall show you someday, you can watch as the humans below us scream, you will love it my sweet dragon." She said, reaching a hand towards my cheek, softly stroking it.

I pulled my blade up, peeling her fingers away from my skin. Her face dropped, surprised. She retreated slowly, her hand hovering in front of her, her face blanched. Her whole body soon started to shake with fury.

"Something wrong, mother?"

"You!" She screamed, launching across the table and wrapping her hands around my throat. Wrong move. She had forgotten, I am the dragon and I'm holding a dagger.

Elle

Feeling time tick by is a new kind of torture. So agonisingly slow. Emmet sat against the wall, my head resting comfortably in his lap. "Will you change your name?" I asked.

"I guess I have an opportunity to do so. Emmari is a distant memory, someone I could have been had my dad been the one to raise me. But it would have been under pretence as my brother was still with me." He said, considering his options.

"Then there's Emmet, strange as it is, I feel no attachment to the name. Until you, no one had used it other than me. I don't know what I would change too."

My hand met his soft chin, lightly tugging his lips to mine.

"Perhaps our next adventure shall help you find it," I said, sighing against his mouth. His soft lips traced mine, time falling away completely. My arms entangled round his neck, hands folding into his hair as I pulled myself closer to him.

His lips eagerly met mine again, his arms hooking under mine and pressing my chest to his. This feeling is so addictive, I was so lost in the feeling that I almost missed the dragon's cry vibrating through the walls of the castle.

Chapter 15

We were alert and rose to our feet instantaneously. Pacing to and fro around the room, straining our ears for any hint of what had happened. But nothing else came through the cracked wood.

"He's ok. He's ok…" Emmet repeated to himself as he hung his head in his hands, too much time had passed since we heard the cry.

"We should never have given him that vial, we should have waited. Created a better plan together, so we could all help." My heart broke at the emotion in Emmet's voice. I opened my mouth, searching for something to say that would help him, soothe him, but the door lock clicked open.

I gave myself whiplash, twirling my head around so fast to the door and watching as a tired, bloodied Matias walked through it. Stepping back, I made room for the brothers to embrace each other.

"How much of it is yours?" I asked, not bothering to avoid his blood-soaked shirt as he squeezed his arms around me.

"Not enough," he replied, stepping back.

"Is she-"

"Dead? Yes. Through her own fault funnily enough, dove straight onto the end of this pointy stick," he explained, throwing his dagger between our feet.

"We heard you, your dragon. We thought you had been hurt, we were so worried," I said, double checking he had no wounds.

Emmet picked up the blade, feeling the weight in his hands.

"She screamed when she realised what we had done, and it alerted the guards outside the room. They were too late, but still loyal to the very end. I fought with them, I killed some, but most fled the castle."

I watched as his eyes flickered to that of his brothers, gazing intently as the memory played out. Emmet offered his hand to me, and I took it, I joined the flashback of images rolling through his mind, I watched as Isla died. Matias returned after the fight with her creatures, standing over her still warm body and watched as her eyes glossed over.

My empty hand found his, hoping to offer a fraction of comfort. The memory faded away leaving the three of us hand in hand, our circle forming around the lump of pain and loss. "Where is father?" Emmet asked.

Matias pinched the bridge of his nose, his eyes closing with such an exasperated cry he dropped to his knees in anguish. Emmet's thoughts pushed into my mind as he joined his brother.

'Father will be okay, he is resting. He got in the middle of the fight with me and one of the creatures, he got wounded but he will heal. Hopefully, he will be able to heal from all the trauma our mother has inflicted upon him,' Matias mused.

I left both brothers embracing, after a quick kiss to their heads. My feet guided me and with each step I felt an immense amount of relief. We would all have a lot to unpack in the coming days, not to mention a huge decision to make. Every day I stayed in this realm, I felt my body become weaker. I missed my mother, and I needed to know if she was okay without me, she was barely coping before I left. Not to mention, Fester... I could not imagine where his mindset was. But I did wish him the best, all the same.

I snapped from my thoughts as my toes crashed into a door, looking around I recognised where I was. "This is her hall of portals."

Their father hobbled into view, leaning on a cane.

"Something about the magic being stronger on the north side of the castle," he explained. That makes sense, I could feel it more here than the throne room.

"Should you not be resting?" I asked, offering my shoulder to lean on.

"I cannot waste what precious time I may have left sitting around and feeling sorry for myself. I have two boys who need their father," he said with a wink, before trailing towards the stairs. This man is a hero.

So, behind this door is a portal that is calling to me. Perhaps it is a way home?

Does Emmet want to return? After all, his family is here. I wonder how his human body is reacting to this place.

"Not very well," he sighed, arms circling my waist.

The others appeared behind him, and we walked together into the foyer of the castle.

"What now? I asked.

Everyone chuckled.

"Someone must take care of this place, there is more to this realm than meets the eye. But Isla was right about something, this is no place for humans like you. The ones in the village below were born here, they have come to grow used to the poison within the air. But you have not. You will need to leave, however, Matias may visit you at any point. He has access to the portals, you will find each other again." His father sighed, resting against his sons. I took a mental picture, tucking it away for a rainy day.

"I suppose that makes you a king brother," Emmet said, the amusement returning to his voice. It had never sounded sweeter.

"On the wind, or in fire and ice, we walk together. That will be true no matter how far away we end up," Matias said.

We came together, hands clasped and foreheads touching.

"I will miss you brother. When everything is in order, please come and visit, I would like to get to know you better," Emmet responded, embracing his brother for a final time.

With a nod, he went and sat beside his father, giving us a moment of privacy. "Please, follow me."

Matias looped our arms, guiding me into an empty room. A fire burned brightly, the only light facing a large, cushioned chair. Bookshelves lined the walls from floor to ceiling, completely empty. "Elle I..." He was at a loss for words.

Sitting down, I patted the space next to me, the fire instantly warmed me from my toes to my knees.

"Elle, I knew from the moment we met you that Emmet was your mate, and not me. But over the years whilst we waited and searched for you, I still had hope that you would be mine, but even more I hoped you'd be our saving grace. You have been so much more."

He touched my hands, drawing my body to face him. Tears hotter than the fire spilled down my cool cheeks.

"I know, or at least I'm sure you know, that letting that part of connection with my brother go was the hardest thing possible. As I lost my only extension to you. But even when you are gone, I will still care," he said, his eyes distant.

I opened my mouth to speak.

"Please, let me finish whilst I have the nerve. I care for you Elle, immensely. With that comes a great amount of respect. You and Emmet fill the empty space in my heart and that will never change. I love you and I hope you will accept me as your family, as a friend, even after everything."

"I love you too Matias, do not ever forget that you are my family. Emmet and I will be one portal hop away," I sobbed, squeezing as tightly as I could around him. He gently pulled back, silver lined the outer ring of his eyes.

"I made this for you, one for you and one for Emmet. They match the one I made for myself," he chuckled.

He opened up his hand and presented me with two matching bracelets.

"When I wear it, I shall think of you."

With one last hug, we said goodbye.

Epilogue

Emmet said goodbye to his father, who I learned was called Arthur. His eyes met mine, as Matias and I walked in, hand in hand.

"This is it," I said.

"So many questions answered, but so many more made," he chuckled.

"You will make a wonderful king, I do not doubt that you will have everything in order very soon," Emmet said. Joining hands, one last time, we repeated, "On the wind, or in fire and ice, we walk together."

Together we walked, exhausted, up the stairs and towards the door calling to me.

"Here we go, back to the place that it all began," I sighed.

"Are you ready for that?" Emmet asked.

"I have no idea," I said, smiling up at him.

But as long as I'm with you... His smirk grew.

Pulling the knob, the heavy door shifted and groaned as it did. A kaleidoscope of colours blinded our eyes, we turned towards our newfound family and waved goodbye.

"I can't wait for you to meet my mother one day, both of you. She will love you, just like me and Emmet do." I said pointedly. Arthur chuckled, the sound much like his sons.

"We shall see you soon," Matias said.

"In no time at all," Emmet echoed.

Hands clasped, we kept our eyes on them, taking one last breath of mossy air before stepping backwards and thinking of home.

Sun beat down on my face, birds singing sweetly in my ears. I opened my eyes, ready to be greeted home. Surprisingly, our eyes met an unfamiliar sight. Emmet pulled me close, our hearts racing.

"What the-"